Insect-Eaters!

Heather Hammonds

CONTENTS

NELSON

THOMSON LEARNING

Australia · Canada · Mexico · Singapore · Spain · United Kingdom · United States

Carnivorous Plants

Most plants need water, sunshine and **healthy** soil to grow.

But some plants live in **poor** soil.

These plants grow by
eating insects and
other little animals.
These plants are called
carnivorous plants.

3

Traps!

Carnivorous plants have leaves that are traps!

Some carnivorous plants have leaves that look like flowers.
Insects land on them.
Then they are trapped!

Some carnivorous plants
have leaves that are sticky.
The insects get stuck!

Sweet and Sticky Traps

The top of this plant is shiny with **nectar**. Hungry insects stop to drink the nectar.

Then they fall inside the plant and cannot get out!

6

Insects fall in the trap.

A pitcher plant

This plant has lots of sticky **tentacles** on its leaves.
Insects land on the tentacles and get stuck!

8

The sticky leaves of this plant trap insects, too.

A butterwort plant

9

Clever Traps

The leaves of this plant
shut when an insect
walks inside them.
Then the plant eats
the insect.
The insect shell
is left behind.

A Venus flytrap

The leaves look like
little balloons.

A bladderwort plant.

This plant has leaves
that look like little balloons.

When an insect
goes near a balloon,
the trap opens
and sucks it inside!

Your Own Insect-Eater!

It is safe to own
an insect-eating plant!

Put it near a window.
Give it lots of water.
It will catch lots
of insects for you!

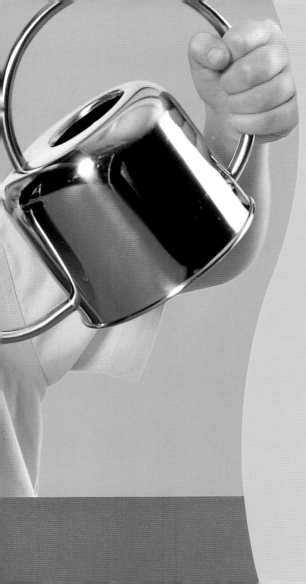

True or False?

1 Insect-eating plants are called:
- cactus plants
- carnivorous plants
- vegetables

2 Insect-eating plants live in:
- sand
- healthy soil
- poor soil

Glossary

carnivorous (say *car-niv-or-us*) eats flesh

healthy full of goodness

nectar a sweet, sticky juice that plants make

poor not healthy

tentacles long, thin parts of a plant that act as arms or fingers

Index